Antigone X

Multimedia variations on a 21st-century view
of the classical play

By

Paula Cizmar

D1737711

NoPassport Press

Cover design: Jonathan Torres.

NoPassport Press
PO Box 1786, South Gate, CA 90280 USA
NoPassportPress@aol.com, www.nopassport.org

First Edition. ISBN: 978-1-387-69222-4

NoPassport

NoPassport is a theatre alliance & press devoted to live, virtual and print action, advocacy and change toward the fostering of cross-cultural and aesthetic diversity in the arts.

NoPassport Press' Dreaming the Americas Series and Theatre & Performance PlayTexts Series promotes new writing for the stage, texts on theory and practice and theatrical translations.

NoPassport is a sponsored project of Fractured Atlas. Tax-deductible donations to NoPassport to fund future publications, conferences and performance events may be made directly to
https://www.fracturedatlas.org/site/fiscal/profile?id=2623

Antigone X

Multimedia variations on a 21st-century view
of the classical play

A Play

By

Paula Cizmar

The X of *Antigone X*

An interview with playwright Paula Cizmar
by Jeff Janisheski

Jeff: My first question is, why *Antigone*? Why now?

Paula: It was a convergence of the times, minds, and needs. Dean David Bridel wanted me to write an adaptation of *Antigone* for the MFA Acting class at USC's School of Dramatic Arts. I took the project on before the election. After the election the play became even more urgent in terms of why it should exist now: it's about a woman standing up to an authority she knows is wrong. This is what has made it endure for over 2,000 years.

When I first started to write I was plagued by the idea of so many people trying to escape from civil war in their homeland – going across the water on boats and washing up dead on the shores of islands in the middle of the Mediterranean. So, these ideas of civil war, of not being safe in your own country, of standing up to unjust power, of being a refugee and a leftover of war – all of those were really powerful impulses when I started this play.
But as I continued, it became more important for it to be about standing up to an authoritarian leader who isn't making sense anymore. What's really interesting about Creon is that when you first hear him in the play he almost sounds reasonable: there's just been a war, he wants to restore law and order, and everybody is afraid and wants to put their safety in the hands of someone who says, "I'm strong and I will take care of you."

But what starts to happen, of course, is that power corrupts him. And the idea that somebody is going to take a stand against that corrupt power is truly important. That is what draws people to this play. And the fact that it was a woman was really important, especially after the 2016 election. It became clear to me with the various Women's Marches that women had to lead a resistance against a leader who was making no sense and didn't value them. While this play is not designed to be a response to the current government, it certainly is a response to authoritarianism anywhere.

Jeff: The different aspects of resistance in the play are only gaining more relevance and meaning with the current administration – in terms of #MeToo and other resistance movements erupting.

Paula: Exactly. When I started the play, I think we all assumed that Hillary Clinton was going to win the election. So, the notions of rising up to authoritarianism or rising up against a demagogue were more abstract. But now it's embodied in the flesh with our current president. The resistance that Antigone instigates – and the resistance that a lot of women now are trying to cling to – is a direct result of the current president that we have: it's aimed against that mindset and that kind of baseless and nonsensical authoritarianism. So, yes, it's a play about resistance and I think that focus sharpened after the election.

Jeff: After the 2016 election, how did you reshape the play?

Paula: The play became angrier.

I started off with the play being more melancholy and regretful because what was really plaguing me were those images of refugees in tiny boats in the middle of the Mediterranean, images of the bodies of drowned refugees washing up on shores. What was most prevalent in my mind at the time was that people will go to incredibly desperate measures to escape war and oppression. But after the election, I was so incredibly fed up – not only with the person we elected but with the American public and their lack of awareness of what was going on and what they had allowed to happen – that I was just in a state of rage. So, after the election I sat down and put an angrier spin on the play: it became about resisting this *nonsense.*

Jeff: Can you talk about some of the important dramaturgical interventions and changes you've injected into the script? For example, the figure of Ismene (Esme) returning at the end.

Paula: Well, among other things, I made Tiresias female. But yes, the character of Ismene was really important to me, so I called her Esme to make the distinction that she's not the Ismene you know from the original.

I wanted to investigate why Ismene disappears in Sophocles' play. Why does Antigone say there's no one left to mourn her, or Creon say there's no one left? Why do they keep forgetting Esme? And why do we remember the sister who resists and the other one is a forgotten figure? Ismene was with Oedipus when he put himself into exile.

9

She was there and yet she gets forgotten and neglected. So, I wanted to examine why: is it strictly the ego of Antigone or is Antigone trying to downplay her sister's participation so that Esme will be protected and someone from the family will survive?

Esme is the person who was always there to support her family; she had to go through the same insane problems that Antigone did and endure the same humiliation of being from that family that Antigone had to – and yet she doesn't get credit or recognition. But Esme is not going to let the family die: her resistance at the end of *Antigone X* is a way of carrying on her sister's torch, of showing that the battle isn't over.

I wanted Esme to be linked to the resistance because it's not going to stop. If you strike one of us down, another one will stand up in her place. We just can't stop. The play might be over, but there's work to be done.

Jeff: Is that why you changed the name from Ismene to Esme? So that her identity shifts in your play compared to Sophocles'?

Paula: Yes. I kept with the basic personality traits of all the other characters except for Ismene. Hence, I changed her to Esme. I wanted it to be close enough so it was recognizable. But I wanted it to be absolutely clear: this is not the old Ismene, this is a different character. She's not to be forgotten, she's not to be left behind.

Jeff: You've talked about how some feminist scholars – like Bonnie Honig in her book *Antigone Interrupted* – have suggested that Ismene actually did help Antigone bury the body.

Paula: Right, because there are certain ritual elements that had to happen – like the lifting of the body. The argument is that Antigone could not have done that alone and her sister was there helping her. Originally, I wanted to make that explicit: that Esme helped with the burial and Antigone wanted her to be quiet so at least one of them would survive. So, it's a moment of Antigone being selfless for a change.

But after a while I didn't want to overtly state it; I wanted to leave it up to the audience to decide. Did Antigone work alone or did she have help?

Jeff: The other thing that shifts dramaturgically is that Sophocles' original – despite being called *Antigone* – is really Creon's play. But what I loved about your adaptation is how you end with Esme.

Paula: That was intentional. From the very beginning, when I decided to change Ismene's name I also decided that she was going to end the play. She represents the future. And I wanted her to end the play with the line "This isn't over," which can be read in multiple ways: as a threat, a warning or a promise. And it was important to me that the play shift away from being Creon's play. I wanted there to be attention paid to the fact that the chief mover and shaker in this play – the one who creates all the trouble and stands up to power – is Antigone.

Jeff: Why the X in *Antigone X*?

Paula: X is always the unknown. X is the thing you're solving for in an equation. X also represents every man, every woman, everybody. X is the collective. X allows somebody to not be claimed by any one particular group or family or clan. Thus, she's Antigone X. She could be anyone – from any time, any era, any place.

Sophocles wrote his play about a specific time and specific characters that were important to the Greeks. But the play has survived for over 2,000 years. I wanted to pay some kind of homage to the fact that this play is ancient but also contemporary. To put that X in there creates a place that's not nailed down. The X is the unknown, but it's also everything. It's got a connotation of belonging and connecting to a larger thing.

Jeff: I was reading your other plays, and there are three threads I've picked out. The first is a commitment to poetic or heightened language in plays like *The Last Nights of Scheherazade*, *Antigone X* and *Strawberry*. The second is a disorienting sense of time and space. The "inner soul" of *Antigone X* is a "jumble of times" and is set in "The present. Or another present." *The Chisera* is set in both the past and present – it switches from 1903 to a parallel story set in the present. And the third thing was how you often shift the play's perspective: shifting the focus of *Antigone X* back to Antigone and Esme, or in your play, *January*, you tell the story through the eyes of the mother whose son has been killed and her assault by the media. Can you talk about those three threads – your use of language, time and perspective?

Paula: Consciously or unconsciously, I have almost always heightened the language in my plays. It's theater. It's not television; it's not the movies. It's more language-based. We don't have beautiful cinematography to transport us to a gorgeous island or a terrifying war zone. The language has to do it.

I like to draw audiences in using that language. It's fun to paint with language. The plays I write are about issues and I am always looking for a way to create characters that are complex and rich, and who you would want to listen to about those issues. So, the language has to be richer than ordinary speech. Their heightened language might take you on a journey; it might transport you into a different state of mind or different state of being.

And I do like to mess around with time and place. Again, we're not writing for television or movies. We can play a little more. Theatre has always been able to have direct address to the audience and acknowledge that they're there and have very fluid time and very fluid space. I love when I go to a play, where there's a dream or vision or nightmare, or there's a rewind and we go back a few scenes and pick up another time and place, and move on. I mostly do these things because they entertain me; it's also really important for playwrights to stake out what theater is. And having that freedom to play with juxtaposing time and that freedom of poetic language is a way to actually turn the limitations of theater into an advantage.

People are going to preach to us over and over again about the poverty of the theater; it's not going to have the bells and whistles of a great big action movie. All of it has to be done with the imagination. And these, to me, are just ways of inviting the audience along on this imaginative journey where we all picture the place and try to kind of create the place and the world together.

In terms of the third thread – about shifting perspectives – that's always exciting to me when I pick up a novel or go to a play or read a poem and perspective shifts. So, changing perspective is just me playing and trying to have some fun with the form, and to create an experience with the plays that's just maybe a little unexpected for the audience: wait, I thought we were on one track and now we're inside the head of someone else, or we're going on a different journey; I didn't expect that.

Jeff: What were your influences as a playwright?

Paula: In college, I always wrote poetry and my intention was to be a poet. I never, ever thought of entering the theater at all. I think it was just the slight detour of working on the campus newspaper that took me to playwriting, and ultimately my playwriting became some kind of weird convergence between poetry and storytelling.

I thought that if I wanted to earn a living as a writer, that it was probably going to have to be some form of journalism. So, I took a practical route and became a reporter briefly. And it was the unearthing of stories, of digging into stories and doing research as a journalist – combined that with my interest in poetry and music – that ultimately converged and created my playwriting style.

Jeff: *Antigone X* seems like a blend of both that poetic impulse and your journalistic impulse. There's so much of the heightened language, the poetry, the evocative imagery; and there's also a clear sense of history and politics that's woven into all the language.

Paula: Yes, one example of that is in the scene in which Antigone describes to Esme what's wrong with this world, and what happens when people go unnamed, unburied and unremembered.

> *All along the border between Mexico and the U.S.,
> bodies lost in the desert, bones stripped clean of
> flesh by buzzards and coyotes—and all they wanted
> was to make their way north. Armenians—
> massacred just because of their religion. Poisoned.
> Burned. Drowned. In Rwanda, skulls of the Tutsi on
> display at the genocide museum. In Treblinka, the
> Nazis knocked down the death camp, covered the
> fields, and made it look like a farm. Death—gone.
> Magic. No evil happened here. In Belarus, in
> Ukraine, a team of grave-hunters knocks on doors
> in remote villages, looking for the elderly. They ask,
> Did you live here during the war? Did you see
> anything? Do you know where the bodies are
> buried? In Basra, 150 bound and blindfolded
> corpses in a mass grave. A football ground in
> Ramadi. A farmer's field in Srebrenica. A million
> bodies in Cambodia. All these souls, wandering
> loose, eternal unrest, no one to build them a
> monument or an altar where they can chant a
> funeral song.*

That is the journalism and the research being married to rhythmic language.

Jeff: That monologue is a phenomenal example of the musicality and poetry of your language. That monologue is so percussive and musical. It builds, has an arc and crescendos. It reminds me of the percussive and musical monologues in Sam Shepard's plays.

Paula: In looking back, I think Shepard was probably my greatest influence. Shepard was very liberating because he basically said, "No, I'm going to do theater this way." And I thought, "Oh, okay." Well, whether I do it his way or not, I knew that I could then do it any way I wanted to.

But it is absolutely imperative to me that the language be rhythmic. I just have this ear and when I hear a line that is off in terms of its rhythm, or when I read a scene that doesn't seem to have an ending that has some kind of rhythmic sense to it at the end, it really disturbs me. It bothers my ear. It's very intuitive and it has to do with sound. Most of my favorite writers were musicians of some kind. They had musical training or played the piano or were rock musicians like Shepard.

Jeff: When we last spoke, you were talking about this being a play about war: the aftermath of war and the psychology of war on people; and how war dehumanizes people and renders them invisible, where identities get erased. And you've added a beginning that brings the brutality of war to the forefront. Can you talk more about those deep concerns of yours and how they're threaded through the play?

Paula: We can't miss the fact in the original *Antigone* that there has just been a war. I've been bothered since 9/11 about America's involvement in wars, our military interventions and invasions overseas. There are countries in the Middle East now that are involved in civil wars that could be part of the destabilizing influence we had as Americans since 9/11.

But the thing that really disturbed me the most was thinking back to who the victims are in these wars. They're almost always the little people who are powerless. They're frequently women and they're often children. I wanted there to be someone who is saying, "Enough." And I think that's what Antigone is doing in this play also. She's saying, "Enough."

Hence that one speech that we were both just talking about. The fact that there are these places all around the world where, after wars or during wars, people have gone missing. It's disturbing to me. And the whole idea of an unmarked grave or mass graves is something that is viscerally disturbing to me.

The longer you're on the planet and the more you read about human atrocities – and the more you learn about mass graves like in Bosnia and Rwanda – the more you understand that this play is deeply disturbing. Because Sophocles was saying, 2,400 years ago, we cannot allow people to become anonymous victims in wars. We can't allow people to go unmarked and unburied.

Antigone's monologue we mentioned is really

about unmarked graves, mass graves and people turning on their own people. It's not just invaders from the outside, but about people killing their own people: people attacking their neighbors and people who are part of their community.

Jeff: What do you want the audience to get out of *Antigone X?*

Paula: At the end of the play, Esme says "And this isn't over." I do want people to understand that you can't be complacent. That you can't assume that people are going to do the right or decent thing. You have to be very careful about who has power and how they wield it. And you have to be prepared to resist.

I was listening to a podcast today about the atrocious treatment of the suffragettes in England who were force-fed in their jail cells when they went on hunger strikes. You think of the atrocities that were committed against people everywhere who just wanted the right to vote or other basic rights and were repressed by their governments.

This play is my anti-authoritarian streak coming out and saying, "Stop it!" I want people to be left with a feeling that they have to do something. It doesn't matter what it is. It can be small. There are going to be people who are going to take direct action, people who will take indirect action and people who will at least just realize that we can't sit back and let other people take care of us. But we have to do something. That's what I would like.

Interviewed on February 12, 2018
Long Beach, CA

About the Author: Paula Cizmar

Paula Cizmar is an award-winning playwright whose work combines poetry and politics and is concerned with the way stories get told in a culture and with who gets left out of the discussion. Her plays have been produced all over the country: Portland Stage, San Diego Rep, The Women's Project (NYC), Cherry Lane (NYC), Jungle Theatre (Minneapolis), Cal Rep, and Playwrights Arena @ LATC. Plays include: *Strawberry*, *Still Life with Parrot & Monkey*, *January*, *The Chisera*, *Candy & Shelley Go to the Desert* and *Street Stories*. She was one of the seven women writers commissioned by Center Theatre Group and Playwrights Arena to write *The Hotel Play*, a site-specific, immersive theatre piece that marked the 25th anniversary of the 1992 Los Angeles uprising; it was produced in guest rooms and on the grounds of the downtown Radisson Hotel. Her many honors include two NEA grants; an international residency at the Rockefeller Study Center in Bellagio, Italy; work selected for Sundance, the O'Neill National Playwrights Conference, and EnVision at Bard; and a TCG/Mellon Foundation On the Road grant. She is one of the writers of the documentary play *Seven*, which has been translated into 20-plus languages and has been produced in over 30 countries to generate dialogue about human rights. She has been awarded numerous commissions and has done adaptations of Sophocles and Lope de Vega. Her play, *The Last Nights of Scheherazade*, won the Israel Baran Award. Also a librettist, she was selected to be part of the Paderewski Cycle, writing the book and lyrics for *Golden*, with music by Nathan Wang. An opera she is writing with composer Guang Yang, *The Night Flight of Minerva's Owl*, was selected for Pittsburgh Festival Opera's Fight for the

Right project. Cizmar Is Associate Professor of Theatre Practice at the University of Southern California School of Dramatic Arts; at USC, she founded the Deep Map Theatre Project, which allows her undergraduate playwrights the opportunity to write and perform pop-up plays about current events issues in a street-theatre style. She is a winner of a Mellon Mentoring Award for Mentoring Undergraduates at USC and has produced three events for USC Visions and Voices: The Arts and Humanities Initiative. For more information, visit www.paulacizmar.net.

About the Director: Jeff Janisheski

Jeff Janisheski is a teacher, arts manager, director and writer. He focuses extensively on international collaborations: over the past twenty years he has taught and directed in Australia, England, Japan, Korea, Russia, Vietnam and the US. He is Professor and Chair of the Theatre Arts Department at California State University, Long Beach where he is also Artistic Director of California Repertory Company (Cal Rep). From 2012-2015 he was Head of Acting at Australia's leading drama school, the National Institute of Dramatic Art (NIDA), where he reshaped the undergraduate acting curriculum. From 2008-2011 Jeff was Artistic Director of the National Theater Institute (NTI) at the Tony Award-winning Eugene O'Neill Theater Center in Connecticut, America's preeminent organization dedicated to the development of new plays and music theatre. From 2004-2008 he was Associate Artistic Director at New York's Classic Stage Company (CSC) where he associate-produced shows featuring Anne Bogart/SITI Company, Alan Cumming, David Ives, Pavol Liska/Nature Theater of Oklahoma, David Oyelowo, John Turturro and Dianne Wiest. He co-founded and co-directed the biennial New York International Butoh Festival; from 2003-2007 he presented the work of over fifty *butoh*-inspired artists from Europe, Japan, South America and the US. A chapter on his approach to actor training will be published in the forthcoming Palgrave book, *The Training and Education of Actors*, which will be an international survey of contemporary theatre training. Jeff holds an MFA in Directing from Columbia University and studied in Japan for over three years with *butoh*'s co-creator Kazuo Ohno. www.jeffjanisheski.com

Antigone X was first produced by the MFA Rep, School of Dramatic Arts, University of Southern California (David Bridel, Dean), at the Scene Dock Theatre, Los Angeles, California, opening on March 1, 2017, with the following cast:

ANTIGONE X: Merhnaz Mohammadi
ESME: Kristina Hanna
CREON: Julian Juaquin
HAEMON: Charles Stern
EURYDICE: Selena Scott-Bennin
TIRESIAS: Courtney Lloyd
HERM: Jim French
ZENO: Ryan Alexander Holmes

Other parts played by the company

Director: Anita Dashiell-Sparks
Scenic Designer: Takeshi Kata
Costume and Mask Designer: Tina Haatainen-Jones
Lighting Designer: Trevor Burk
Projection Designer: Simon Chau
Sound Designer: Stephen Jensen
Fight Choreographer: Edgar Landa
Vocal Coach: Natsuko Ohama
Stage Manager: Alex Rehberger

With special thanks to David Warshofsky and Natsuko Ohama, artistic consultants

Antigone X was produced by Cal Rep/California Repertory Company (Jeff Janisheski, Artistic Director and Chris Anthony, Managing Director) at California State University, Long Beach; opening at the Studio Theatre on March 23, 2018, with the following cast:

ANTIGONE X: Dorthea Darby
ESME: AnnaJane Murphy
CREON: Tom Trudgeon
HAEMON: Malachi Beasley
EURYDICE: Rachel Post
TIRESIAS: Kayla Manuel
HERM: Corduroy Chapman
ZENO: Erin Galloway

Other parts played by the company

Director: Jeff Janisheski
Set Designer: Xiyu Lin
Costume Designer: Maria Huber
Lighting Designer: Caitlin Eby
Video Designer: Hsuan-Kuang Hsieh
Sound Designer/Composer: Yiannis Christofides
Makeup Designers: Haley Fenninger and Maddie Focht
Assistant Directors: Lisa Pelikan, April Sigman-Marx, Katie
        Smithey
Choreographer: Francesca Jandasek
Movement Coach: Ezra LeBank
Voice Coaches: Andrea Caban and Simon Masterton
Stage Manager: Sabrina Loe
Assistant Stage Manager: Chase Niles
Company Manager: Carly Neill

CHARACTERS

ANTIGONE X – Fierce, smart, proud, a bit of a firebrand, not afraid of a fight. Can be blindly stubborn.

ESME – Smart like her sister Antigone but ruled more by reason and love; more willing to engage via indirect methods than overt attack. Yet she is no pushover.

TIRESIAS – Appears in the guise of a beautiful woman; the blind prophet, the soothsayer, the oracle. Tiresias is midway through a 7-year curse, btw, stuck being a female for 3 ½ more years.

EURYDICE – The wife of Creon, queen of Thebes; wants to believe that everything is fine and everyone is going to make the right choice—but then...

CREON – Absolutely powerful. A bit of a demagogue, but then that's OK—because he is always on the right side, right? He rules because he is supposed to and the people want him. Or so he thinks.

HAEMON – Son of Creon. More of a romantic than his father; he is more of an observer of people and capable of seeing the less obvious within them.

HERM THE SENTRY-MESSENGER-GUARD – Smart enough to know when he has to kowtow to authority; capable of playing dumb, playing innocent—to get away with delivering the news that people don't want to hear.

ZENO THE AIDE-DE-CAMP – The one who gets stuck having to deal with all of Creon's awful directives, the one who gets put in charge of the worst possible details. First a yes-man, then...

PLUS: ALL ACTORS DOUBLE AS CHORUS MEMBERS, playing numerous smaller roles, including refugees, soothsayers, wailers, soldiers, a boy. Birds, wild dogs. Frenzied dancers. They could even be the wind.
Note: The cast should be a mix of races, ethnicities; it is also entirely fine to cast additional actors for some of the choral scenes. It is also possible to do the play with an all-female cast.

TIME: The present. Or another present.

PLACE: A refugee camp outside the ruined city of Thebes—which could be in any country, any continent. It is dangerous. Reduced to rubble. Volatile.

A NOTE ABOUT THEATRICALITY, ETC.: This is intended to be a play that is free, flexible, imaginative, not particularly rooted in reality. And it is open to many kinds of production interpretations. Video, enhanced sound, movement, and dance—all are welcome and even expected. If there are projections and enhanced new media additions—wonderful. If the choral sections are done by one actor at a time, or multiple voices at the same time, or if they even become sung pieces, that's also great. If movement and dance enhance these sections—fabulous. Nothing is intended to be rooted in any particular time, any particular place, any particular culture. War, chaos, imbalance of power, revenge, and grief are for all time. The casting should suggest this—with actors of all races and ethnicities playing the roles. The costumes don't need to specify time or gender. For example, the soldiers could be in camouflage or the outfit of an ancient Greek warrior or an Amazon or a street fighter or all of the above. The wailers could be in black robes and hoods reminiscent of Medieval monks, or loose black dresses, or jeans and hoodies, or burkas, or habits, or wrapped in long shawls. Or they could just be in tattered clothing of the current day. Instead of black they could be clothed in white. The entire cast could be in jeans and hoodies all the time. The soldiers could be female, the wailers could be male. What is important is: They have seen brutality, they have seen injustice, their homes are gone, they live in ruins, and they have no power.

The artists working on this piece are invited to play with the idea of timelessness of these themes and expand and imagine. And, of course, to remember that this is theatre. We already know it isn't real—we just want to reach out and touch someone with whatever we create.

Come out of the twilight
and walk before us a while,
friendly, with the light step
of one whose mind is fully made up, terrible
to the terrible.

You who turn away, I know
how you feared death, but
still more you fear
unworthy life.

And you let the powerful get away
with nothing, and did not reconcile yourself
with the obfuscators, nor did you ever
forget affront, and let the dust settle
on their misdeeds.

I salute you!

Bertolt Brecht, *Antigone*

.

PROLOGUE: WAR OF WARS

Darkness.   An army marches.
They are not soldiers from any one particular time.
They make the noise of 10,000.
*The stomping of boots, the **breathing** in unison.*
The war chant. It's as if they are tanks.

Helicopters. Deafening noises of war.

A stylized ritualistic battle. It could be movement
only. A dance.
Or a choreographed fight with swords, knives, fists,
guns.
It needs to be brutal. And scary.

The battle, the breathing, all the noises blend.
We may even hear WAILERS.
Bombs bursting. Fire. Signal flares.

Then it all stops. In the smoke of war, we see a body.
Lying on the battlefield. Alone. In a pool of blood.

Suddenly: A flash of bright white light.

A squad of SOLDIERS marches in formation, doing a
cadence call. Sing-song rhythms.

SOLDIER 1: The radiant glories of victory

    SOLDIERS: The radiant glories of victory

SOLDIER 1: Were paid for with our bravery

SOLDIERS: Were paid for with our bravery

The cadence gives way to a telling of the battle. Still marching, the soldiers tell the story together, sometimes in unison, sometimes trading off lines.

SOLDIER: We have won, beat back the armies of Argives

SOLDIER: Or whoever they were

SOLDIER: No one likes a loser

SOLDIER: No one likes a braggart

SOLDIER 1: The radiant glories of victory

SOLDIERS: Were paid for with our bravery

SOLDIER: In the heat of day the enemy

ALL SOLDIERS: Wiped out

SOLDIER: From overhead

SOLDIER: Drones, helicopters

SOLDIER: White-shielded saviors swooping out of the sky

SOLDIER: Come to liberate

SOLDIER: Come to devastate

SOLDIER: Their golden eagles

SOLDIER: Sent from the gods

SOLDIER: Gleaming in the sun as the bombs go

SOLDIERS: Boom Boom Boom

SOLDIER: Snipers on rooftops

SOLDIER: The blinding light of righteousness

SOLDIER: Bombs raining down—on whoever was unlucky enough to be out in the street

SOLDIER: Until it all comes down to just two brothers
One against another
Fighting
Until the day fades

> *Darkness now descends, along with the smoke of war.*

SOLDIER: Fighting until one wins

SOLDIER: Who wins?

SOLDIER: Both are dead, one side wins

SOLDIER: But who are the winners
And what is the victory
And where are we anyway
Boom   Boom   Boom

> *The soldiers stop marching. All about them is ruin. Bombed out craters from buildings. Smoke.*

> *Everything blown to oblivion. Refugees of war emerge from the smoke and darkness.*

SOLDIER: Set up the camps!   Get these people out of the open—

SOLDIER: Get these people into camps!

A soldier grabs a bullhorn or emergency loudspeaker:

SOLDIER: Attention—If your home has been destroyed, if you are in exile, report to a refugee camp now. Repeat: Report to a refugee camp now!

Confusion. In the dark of night, the Refugees, lit by only a pale moon, create the merest suggestion of an encampment. Hints of tents, tarps, tattered cloth flapping in the wind—a reminder of billowing sails.

SCENE. THE CALL.

In darkness, a desperate, frenzied ANTIGONE pulls her sister ESME past the refugees, through the encampment. Antigone drags Esme through the ruins to a remote area.

ANTIGONE: Let's go let's go there there—

ESME: We're not supposed to be outside the c—

ANTIGONE: Come—

ESME: Suppose someone sees—

ANTIGONE: Moon. Hiding behind the clouds—. Mist—

ESME: Suppose someone hears us—

ANTIGONE: Quick. What do you know?

ESME: The curfew—

ANTIGONE: Tell me—

ESME: If we get caught—

ANTIGONE: —Sun won't be up for hours—

ESME: Shh. I just—listen—something out there—

She listens—is there a distant sound?

ANTIGONE: There's nothing.

ESME: Men prowling coyotes jackals scavenging   people out hunting for—.

ANTIGONE: Shh.

ESME: They're desperate they're out of their heads they'd like nothing more than to get their paws on—

ANTIGONE: Tell me what you know.

ESME: Me? Nothing.

ANTIGONE: Tell me.

ESME: I know our brothers are dead.

ANTIGONE: Go on.

ESME: And every cell in my body, any place I could feel something—it's empty.

ANTIGONE: Say what you heard.

ESME: What, that they killed each other? Savagely? One brother killing another. That's all I know. It's enough.

ANTIGONE: Nothing else.

ESME: No. Why?

ANTIGONE: He is trying to humiliate us.

ESME: He?

ANTIGONE: If he shames us, he controls us. And then he answers to no one.

ESME: I don't—

ANTIGONE: You really didn't hear? They say Creon will give our brother Eteocles the burial of a warrior. Roses—however he will find them in this place, there will be roses. Wine—as if there is a drop to be had. Mourners. Funeral songs. He will be hailed as a patriot. He will have a hero's grave. For all eternity.

ESME: Eteocles deserved nothing less.

ANTIGONE: And Polynices?

ESME: Both our brothers will sleep forever. Eternal rest. The earth owns them.

ANTIGONE: No—

ESME: But—

ANTIGONE: —I heard Creon will force Polynices to go unburied, unmourned, exposed for all to see.

ESME: Who told you that?

ANTIGONE: He will lie dead. In the open. He will be food for vultures, for anything wild that crawls or drops out of the sky. Food for the starving dogs ravaging the streets.

ESME: Someone is just scaring y—

ANTIGONE: He will be torn to pieces. He will be consumed before our very eyes. He will be ripped apart before the blow flies can lay eggs in his eyes and bone beetles nest in the folds of his skin and maggots crawl out of his ears—

ESME: No!

ANTIGONE: People all over the camp—that's what they're saying—

ESME: Creon is our uncle. He wouldn't.

ANTIGONE: They're saying he promises death to anyone who tries to move the body. Death to anyone who mourns him. Who gives him an honorable burial.

ESME: Just. Crazy talk—

ANTIGONE: He calls Polynices a traitor.

ESME: He—.

ANTIGONE: What.

ESME: Nothing.

ANTIGONE: You think it's true.

ESME: I can't think my head is aching my heart is bursting my eyes hurt just stop stop

ANTIGONE: They were both warriors.

ESME: Stop.

ANTIGONE: They would both be alive today.

ESME: If.

ANTIGONE: If Eteocles would have lived up to his end of the bargain. If he had shared power with Polynices, given him his time in charge. If he had followed our father wishes—

ESME: Alright. Yes. Eteocles should have stepped down— but Polynices went too far. He brought outsiders into the fight.

ANTIGONE: He couldn't fight alone.   He wanted victory over an oppressor—

ESME: An oppressor who was your brother—your kin.   Not an outside invader who doesn't care if you live or die.

ANTIGONE: Polynices was fighting to right a wrong—

ESME: Righting a wrong with wrong?   Righting a wrong for who?

ANTIGONE: He was trying to protect us.

ESME: Foreign soldiers raping women and girls so-called rebels putting rifles into the hands of little boys filling their heads with hate marching old men into pits taking our land calling it theirs

ANTIGONE: He had to have allies

ESME: We would have been wiped out!

> *Beat.*

ANTIGONE: And look at us now.

> *Beat.*

Do you know the difference between a human being—a once-breathing body now lifeless—and a filth-stinking rot-oozing blood-blackened heap of garbage?

ESME: Don't speak of the dead that way.

ANTIGONE: That is the way he will leave our brother. For all to see.

ESME: They all see us as damaged goods anyway.   Our father is our brother.   Our brother-father killed his own father. Our mother killed herself. Our father-brother ripped out his own eyes and wandered alone like a beggar—

ANTIGONE: Not alone. I was with him.

ESME: And me.

ANTIGONE: Yes, you were there too.

ESME: You always forget. I don't. I don't forget that our mother had a husband who was her son. Cursed! And her first husband a rapist, and his father ripped apart by—

ANTIGONE: I don't care how it happened! I don't care how it started! How far back do we have to go to see who was right in a thousand-year-old war?

ESME: Right again.

ANTIGONE: And now we are being humiliated. Wiped out.

ESME: They're all dead. But we are still here.

ANTIGONE: If Creon has his way—we are broken. That's how he wipes us out. Invisible like the homeless under the bridge.

ESME: We're all homeless now. There is no bridge.

ANTIGONE: Shamed, as if we are thieves.

ESME: I can live with shame. I can be invisible.

ANTIGONE: Maybe you can. Not me.

> *A noise is heard.*

Shhh.

ESME: Go!

> *They scramble out of sight. Noise—perhaps a rustling wind. Way off in the distance, a little gunfire here and there. An odd light—a flare of some kind. Spooky—but far off.*

*In the darkness, we can barely make out the
makeshift refugee camp. EURYDICE enters, whistling
for her dog, calling softly.*

EURYDICE: Dog. Sweet doggie. Little pet. Come here.
Come.

A SOLDIER rushes on, following her.

SOLDIER: My lady. Beloved Queen. Eurydice.

EURYDICE: Oh. Yes.

SOLDIER: You shouldn't be out here, ma'am.

EURYDICE: The sun seems slow to rise today.

SOLDIER: It does.

EURYDICE: When daylight comes—well. We'll have to be
patient. Have you seen my husband?

SOLDIER: He's tending to some mop-up operations,
ma'am.

EURYDICE: Oh?

SOLDIER: A pocket of rebels here and there. Some in the
hills.

EURYDICE: I have questions for him. Things to do.

SOLDIER: Nothing to worry about.

EURYDICE: And my pup—my little dog—has anyone seen
my little dog? Odd isn't it? With the coming dawn I expect

the sweet songs of birds.   And yet, today. Silent.   I'm sure they'll start

SOLDIER: Yes ma'am.

EURYDICE: Will there be a celebration?

SOLDIER: Ma'am?

EURYDICE: Of our triumph. There should be dancing, don't you think?

SOLDIER: Yes, ma'am.

EURYDICE: Praise for what we have done.

SOLDIER: My queen.

The soldiers' cadence is heard again, approaching.

SOLDIER: The radiant glories of victory

    SOLDIERS: The radiant glories of victory

The voices grow closer.

SOLDIER: Were paid for with our bravery—

The faint gunfire in the distance gives way to helicopter noises. Deafening. The helicopters pass overhead. Then the approach of drums and cheers.

The drums grow closer.

SCENE. REALITY OF THE COMING DAY

*It is still dark. A procession of military enters—
followed by CREON and his aide-de-camp, ZENO.*

*Creon acknowledges Eurydice—brings her to the
front of the crowd. He turns to face his people.*

CREON: Soldiers, citizens, all the brave.   Here we are—in the almost dawn. I did not want to wait even one more hour to tell you: The threat to our freedom is vanquished. The peace is ours.

Yet peace isn't bestowed automatically is it? A grace granted us at birth? Peace has to be won.   Peace has to be fought for.   Peace, yes, we have to die for it.   I honor you for pledging your lives to making our peace.

Now here we are: Secure. Safe. And we vow to be ever watchful so that our peace is never in peril again, so that we do not fear losing our land, our families, our country, our culture. We will be vigilant.

I am here to protect you, to lead you, to govern with true judgment and a firm hand, to root out the problem that lurks amongst us, so that no one gets between us and our way of life, between us and our safety. If any outsider wants to challenge us, I say, Bring it on.

I am not afraid because I have seen what we can do.   We will not bow to threats.   We will stand together. We will not put self or family or any other ties above our loyalty to our country.

Smooth sailing, an upright ship of state—that is what I, your captain, pledge to you.

Law and order—not recklessness and unrest. We know what is needed to set out on our next voyage, to raise our city back up from ashes. A gleaming treasure again. We know what we're sailing toward. Clean streets, safe neighborhoods, open air. We will raise it up. Secure. Why live in fear?

Never let it be said that I don't reward the brave who stood by me, the loyal, the fearless, the heroes. I know who is devoted to our cause. And never let it be said that I will ever allow a traitor to stand side by side with a patriot.

So I say to you now: Eteocles, my nephew, son of your former king, shall be buried with all the sacred rituals, all the ceremony, all the mourners, memorials, and eulogies, all the hymns and songs, that a hero has earned. He will have the highest honors, we will build him a tomb of the finest marble, we will name streets, parks, and schools after him, and we will thank him over and over that he gave his life for our freedom.

His brother—I spit upon his name. Treason, coward, traitor, evil—no word could ever be vile enough to describe him. He will not be buried, he will not be mourned. Let him rot where he fell. Let him be food for whatever filthy creature wants to fill its craw with stinking flesh. Let the crows peck out his eyes. Let the vultures pull out his heart. Let the dogs feast on his limbs. Let the worms spill out of his mouth. Let his blackened blood be a warning to anyone and anything that tries to do us harm. Let the stink of his decay blow across the land if that is what it takes to remind us that we must stand for right and decency and the rule of law.

Don't go soft, my friends.   Don't even begin to pity.   Don't think of some misplaced memory of some time in your childhood you shared with him or some false loyalty to another king.   Because I pledge this to you also: If anyone tries to bury him, if anyone tries to perform the ancient rites or lay the body in the ground, they will be put to death.

I hope you heard me correctly.

We must make up our minds what we stand for.   We must decide, will we let treason breed like vermin in our midst, or will we make our line in the sand?   To patriots, I give my blessing.   To anyone who sides with a traitor, I offer you the chance to join the dead below.

Clear?

SOLDIERS: Clear.

CROWD: Creon!   Creon!   Creon!

> *With a nod, Creon dismisses the crowd.*

> *He huddles with Zeno.*

CREON: Zeno, see that the orders are posted throughout the camp for anyone who doubts my intentions.

ZENO: Yes, Commander.

CREON: And see to it that the guards around the body are the best, with the highest integrity.

ZENO: Already arranged, Commander.

CREON: You know how a little filthy lucre can tempt someone down the wrong road.

ZENO: I don't think anyone dares, sir.

CREON: You'd be surprised what people will do for a bribe.

ZENO: They are weak, sir.

CREON: Especially if the price is right.

> *Zeno heads off. Creon goes from soldier to soldier. Salutes. Etc.*
>
> *Refugees retreat back into the shadows or huddle on the ground.*
>
> *The drums begin again, following Creon as he leaves. Loud, then they start to fade in the distance. Then the helicopter sounds start up. They pass overhead and fly off.*
>
> *A faint glow. TIRESIAS appears at her oracle stone.*
>
> *She lights an offering—blows smoke. Listens.*
>
> *A sudden shriek of birds. Deadly, fierce, bloodthirsty. Excruciatingly loud. Something is not right. Tiresias waves them away.*
>
> *She lights another offering. Same response:*

Birds. Raptors. Ferocious. It's not right.

She waves them off again. She picks up her guide stick, uses it to navigate off. Disappears into darkness.

SCENE. UNDER COVER OF NIGHT

Antigone and Esme creep out of hiding.

ANTIGONE: Godgodgod. It's true—

ESME: How can he—he—we should—we should just go. Right now. Take our chances out there.

ANTIGONE: With what—

ESME: We'll get ready. Look for signs for when it's best to go, when the air feels right, when clouds roll in, if there's a storm. You know those things. Then we'll just leave.

ANTIGONE: Leave. We cannot leave.

ESME: We'll go. In the dark.

ANTIGONE: He will not let us leave.

ESME: Why?

ANTIGONE: Because here we are silent. Out there, we are not.

ESME: We'll just take off—

ANTIGONE: And if we could leave, where would we go?

47

ESME: Anywhere.

ANTIGONE: No one will take us in.   We are a reminder.

ESME: Of what.

ANTIGONE: Think about it. You know the answer.

> *Esme takes this in. As she does, sounds of ocean*
> *waves are heard, faintly, in the distance. Then louder.*

ESME: Listen.

ANTIGONE: Is there someone—

ESME: It's the sea.

ANTIGONE: We can't hear it from here.

ESME: If the wind is right, if the waves are large enough—

> *They listen a moment. Antigone relaxes. She does*
> *hear the ocean. [The refugees themselves may*
> *become the waves...]*

ANTIGONE: You have a way of making things better.
Sweet sister.

ESME: You hear it?

ANTIGONE: Now I do.

ESME: Water water water, forever. Blue deep green bluer.
The horizon—the sun's bed.   Waves, little curls of white,
teasing the shore. White stones sea glass aqua pale green

ANTIGONE: Dolphins, off the coast. It would be nice to see them again.

ESME: Suppose. Suppose we slip out of this ruin. Suppose we slip down to the sea. Get on a boat. Sail somewhere.

ANTIGONE: That's a nice dream.

ESME: People have done it.

ANTIGONE: People have been swallowed by the waves.

ESME: Someone will guide us.

ANTIGONE: If we pay them—

ESME: So we'll pay—

ANTIGONE: And when the boat is overflowing, or the vessel overturns, or the raft tears apart in the middle of the sea, or we run out of money—then suddenly only the guide has a life jacket.

ESME: Don't you want to go someplace? Where there isn't the smell of decay. Where we don't have to fear looking at the stars at night.

> *Antigone takes this in. [Bodies in the night may move enhancing the scene, as if it is a dream.]*

Where you can marry Haemon.

ANTIGONE: I don't know if that can happen anymore.

ESME: Where there is the possibility of romance.

ANTIGONE: Flowers, songs, dancing. Is that what you want.

ESME: A future. Happiness. I'll be in your wedding.

ANTIGONE: Just.   Be quiet a moment. I'm trying to hear the waves.

>   *Esme begins to quote an ancient poem by Sappho.*

ESME: "The equal of the gods, there he is
This man sitting so near to you..."

ANTIGONE: Don't—

ESME: You love this poem—
"His voice, silver speech-tones
And lovely glittering laughter."

ANTIGONE: Stop with your poetry, your Sappho—

ESME: You know you can see him. Haemon.

ANTIGONE: I can't—

ESME: Conjure him up—

ANTIGONE: Esme—

ESME: Say it with me—

>   *HAEMON appears. A vision. He has eyes only for*
>   *Antigone. She shakes her head, No.*

I'll say it for you.
"Oh feel it, the fluttering inside me,

My beating heart, my body can barely contain it
When I behold him"

*Haemon chants the poem with Esme—choral or
alternating lines.*

ESME/HAEMON: "Even for a moment;
I can't speak;"

ANTIGONE: Please.

ESME/HAEMON: "My tongue, useless, barely a whisper
A fire rages under my skin
My eyes cannot see,
And echoes ring in my ears, thrumming"

*Antigone is getting caught up in the vision. She
draws nearer to Haemon. They touch.*

ESME/HAEMON: "I flush with fever,
And a blood-flush trembling
Lays its hold on me;
Paler than drought-ruined grass am I,
Half dead for madness—"

*Suddenly Antigone breaks away. Gets her resolve
back.*

ANTIGONE: Enough!

Haemon looks at her a moment—then is gone.

Stop it. Nothing you can do. Nothing you can—. Just.
Stop.

ESME: Just a moment of peace—

ANTIGONE: Here is your moment of peace. A lush hillside. Hedgerows, trees bordering a field, velvety green. Grazing sheep.

ESME: Yes. That's ni—

ANTIGONE: —A bone creeps up out of the earth after a rain. Children playing, riding by on their bicycles, notice the odd bloom sprouting from the ground. What could it be?

ESME: Don't—

ANTIGONE: Then another bone. And another. More and more. Just a little digging and the few people left discover the truth. A pit full of victims.

ESME: Please don't—

ANTIGONE: Ethnic cleansing the enemy said. Bodies tossed in—some maybe when they were still alive— covered over with the soil they had farmed. Now reduced to dust, bone, a few fragments of cloth. Maybe they had to even dig their own resting place. Or the disappeared of Argentina—where are they?

In Iran: Khavaran, the Place of the Damned or the Flower Garden, you choose the name—political prisoners thrown again into a ditch, thrown on top of each other like sacks of moldy potatoes, the burial place hidden, their families arrested if they gather to mourn? Go wander the desert and try to find the grave, an official says. Sometimes they give directions, saying to mothers, go pick up your son—

and the poor woman would go there and all that would remain would be ragged bloody clothes or worse, a severed head in a plastic shopping bag.

ESME: Please—

ANTIGONE: All along the border between Mexico and the U.S., bodies lost in the desert, bones stripped clean of flesh by buzzards and coyotes—and all they wanted was to make their way north. Armenians—massacred just because of their religion. Poisoned. Burned. Drowned. In Rwanda, skulls of the Tutsi on display at the genocide museum. In Treblinka, the Nazis knocked down the death camp, covered the fields, and made it look like a farm. Death— gone. Magic. No evil happened here. In Belarus, in Ukraine, a team of grave-hunters knocks on doors in remote villages, looking for the elderly. They ask, Did you live here during the war? Did you see anything? Do you know where the bodies are buried? In Basra, 150 bound and blindfolded corpses in a mass grave. A football ground in Ramadi. A farmer's field in Srebrenica. A million bodies in Cambodia. All these souls, wandering loose, eternal unrest, no one to build them a monument or an altar where they can chant a funeral song.

> *Esme takes this in. But doesn't speak. [The chorus may be the bodies in this section.]*

ANTIGONE: You know what we have to do.

ESME: I don't know anything.

ANTIGONE: Say what we have to do.

53

ESME: We can do nothing.

ANTIGONE: Shall our brother be reduced to less than human?

ESME: I don't know what you mean.

ANTIGONE: He deserves all the rituals. The burial. The offerings to the gods.

ESME: Our uncle has forbidden it.

ANTIGONE: What is that to us?

ESME: We are alive. Period.

ANTIGONE: Are we?

ESME: What good are we to Polynices if we are dead?

ANTIGONE: What good are we if we don't honor our obligations, if we don't follow a higher law?

ESME: But to die—

ANTIGONE: We don't have long here on earth. But the dead—we're with them forever. We owe them.

ESME: Don't ask me. Please. I. Don't ask me.

ANTIGONE: Fine. I won't ask.

ESME: Your heart is on fire, and my veins fill with ice.

ANTIGONE: I said I won't ask.

ESME: Don't look at me like that.

ANTIGONE: I can't see you right now. Only a ghost.

ESME: Don't do that to me.

ANTIGONE: I have an obligation—

ESME: Don't tell anyone. Keep it quiet. Don't—

ANTIGONE: I'm going to tell the world.

ESME: No no ok ok bury him but for god's sake don't tell anyone—

ANTIGONE: It's fine. You choose life. I choose death.

ESME: Don't do this.

ANTIGONE: We don't need to meet again.

ESME: What? No, you're all I have left, what are you saying?

ANTIGONE: Stop caring about me. Stop thinking of me at all. That will make it easier.

Antigone starts off.

ESME: Wait! No—

ANTIGONE: I have stopped loving you.

ESME: No—Antigone—Stop—

Antigone goes. Esme tries to stop her. Tries to follow her. Loses her.

No no you don't know what you're saying you're just saying this to you don't know what you're doing stop stop come back wait I will never stop loving you you will always be my sister Antigone!

The screech of birds. The roar of wind. Esme is alone.

SCENE.   THE ETERNAL DARK

A cemetery. Though it looks much like the refugee encampment. Or more to the point, the refugee camp looks much like a cemetery.

Off in the distance could be little flickers of light where various illicit sellers ply their wares—whether they're selling black market goods, sex, drugs, etc. Two of these entrepreneurs have set themselves up as SOOTHSAYERS—crystal ball, tarot cards, yarrow sticks, I Ching coins, palm reading, all of it.

SOOTHSAYER 1: Get your fortune, here.

SOOTHSAYER 2: Got your future in the palm of your hand.

In the shadows, a refugee may hold out a palm or throw the I Ching coins. Tiresias, with her long walking stick, is led on by BOY. She sniffs the air.

TIRESIAS: Be my eyes.

BOY: It's dark, sir.

TIRESIAS: That's the point.

BOY: Can't we do this in daylight?

TIRESIAS: What? And have me seen like this?

BOY: You're beautiful, Mr. Tiresias, sir.

TIRESIAS: That's not the point. (beat) But thank you. (beat) You really think so?

BOY: What my mom would call a natural beauty.

TIRESIAS: Oh would she? *(beat)* Stop kissing up. Be my eyes.

BOY: There's no one.

TIRESIAS: Don't fool me.

BOY: Just dark.

TIRESIAS: I can smell them.

BOY: And more dark.

TIRESIAS: Be my eyes.

> *They walk on. Boy tries to avoid the soothsayers, but Tiresias is onto him. She reaches out her stick, taps Soothsayer 1.*

TIRESIAS: What's this? Palm readings? Tarot?

SOOTHSAYER 1: Got a dollar. Step right up. Bones, bucks, clams, ducats, fins, whatever you got.

SOOTHSAYER 2: Two for the price of one over here. I ain't gonna be undersold.

Tiresias reaches out her stick. Touches a card.

TIRESIAS: The Death card?!

SOOTHSAYER 2: That'll getcha.

TIRESIAS: Don't even know the meaning of the oracles!

SOOTHSAYER 1: Move on if you ain't got the benjamins.

TIRESIAS: Your phony fortunes foul the air. Ruining the prophecies. I need to speak to the gods.

SOOTHSAYER 1: You're cute, lady.

TIRESIAS: The birds won't give up their messages with this pestilence—

SOOTHSAYER 2: Ha! This one talks to the birds!

TIRESIAS: Boy? Stand back.

BOY: Sir?

Tiresias uses her stick like a sword and slices at the soothsayer's set-up. Tarot cards, coins, crystal balls— all knocked over. Trashed.

SOOTHSAYER 1: What the fuck—

TIRESIAS: The birds thank you--

SOOTHSAYER 2: Crazy cow—

Soothsayer goes for Tiresias. Something—something supernatural—stops him, freezing him in his tracks.

TIRESIAS: Don't hit a lady. It isn't nice.

The soothsayers scramble to pick up their stuff—and escape Tiresias. Boy shudders. Tiresias senses this.

TIRESIAS: Cold, Boy?

BOY: Yes sir.

TIRESIAS: Dark sucks all the heat out of the earth.

BOY: Weird winds come up.

TIRESIAS: That too. The ice-blue light of moon. Wisps of clouds, as if they're running a finger down her face. What a sight. Perfect.

BOY: But you're blind, sir.

TIRESIAS: I know it's there. Spent a hundred years as a man, and now condemned to be a woman. Well, one thing good about that is that now I can see.

BOY: See what, sir.

TIRESIAS: Forget it. Too hard to explain.

BOY: The sun is starting to come up, sir.

TIRESIAS: Black giving way to purple?

BOY: Yes sir.

TIRESIAS: Copper, gold, ruby—that will follow. *(beat)* Get me out of here boy.

BOY: Yes sir.

Boy leads Tiresias away.

SCENE. LIGHT BREAKS

Dawn. The sun faintly starts to appear. A refugee of the camp sees the approaching dawn and starts to do yoga—the Sun Salutation. Singing a haunting, beautiful mantra while going through the yoga pose.

REFUGEE: Om Namo Bhagavate Vasudevaya....
Om Namo Bhagavate Vasudevaya....

The mantra continues. It fills the sky.

Another refugee may join the Sun Salutation, and the pale dawn grows brighter.

Helicopters roar again, breaking up the peaceful moment. Creon enters with Zeno and another soldier—bodyguards. They head to makeshift headquarters.

Suddenly, HERM the messenger enters the encampment, makes a beeline for Creon.

HERM: King! King Creon—

Zeno and the other soldier immediately put their bodies in front of Creon, protecting him.

ZENO: Halt!

SOLDIER: Grab him!

HERM: Get out of my way or I'll just go and because I'd like to go and you'll never know why I'm here because I'm here but I don't want to be here so OK OK, you want me gone, I'll go.

CREON: Who is this?

HERM: I have a name but it's best you don't know it, your honor, because the less you know about me the better, but the more you know about what I know—well that's all the better, too.

CREON: Bring him over here.

HERM: And I know plenty although you could say it's plenty of nothing, but I got stuck with this so here I am.

> *Zeno and the soldier frisk and restrain Herm as Creon addresses him.*

CREON: What's your name?

HERM: And I told them I would hurry but I have to confess—why all of a sudden do I feel like confessing, do we really have confession in our religion, well, god only knows because I ain't darkened the door of any kind of holy temple in god knows how long oh god there I go taking the name of the lord in vain—

ZENO: Out with it—

HERM: Well anyway I said I would hurry because you know how you're supposed to hurry when you have important news—well I didn't hurry, that's the confession—

ZENO: Stand up straight, soldier. Spit it out.

CREON: Call me when you've beat it out of him. Whatever it is he has to say.

Creon starts to head off.

HERM: WAIT! Wait! Sir, commander, chief, my liege, king, captain, wait, I promise I promise, OK, so OK, so here it goes. You know the body.

CREON: What body?

HERM: I hesitate to say his name sir. I think it's just going to make you upset. You know. The body body. The one we're guarding.

CREON: My nephew.

HERM: I ain't saying the name sir, but sure, that one. The one we ain't supposed to bury.

CREON: Go on.

HERM: And the one nobody else is sposed to bury. You know. 'Cause of him being, you know. Not patriotic and all.

CREON: You have 30 seconds to tell me what has happened.

HERM: I can't do this I can't do this I didn't want to do this why do I have to do it—there we were we were all watching the body and then—I don't want to do this—and then we had to draw straws and I got the short straw so I had to come and be the one to deliver the news and if ever I didn't want to do something well this is it and you don't want to hear it so I don't I'll just be gone.

CREON: Ten seconds.

HERM: It's. It's. OK, maybe it was just I dunno a mirage or a trick of the eye or something but no no, no I think that wasn't it, um um OK, someone buried the body.

CREON: What the—. Who—

HERM: Uh uh uh uh

Zeno grabs Herm, twists him by the arm.

ZENO: Speak up you wretched worm weasel or I'll—

CREON: An entire squad of sentries on duty guarding one body and you're telling me that somehow someone managed to bury it—

HERM: I don't know I guess I we were all watching it and the night was bright and odd and the little meteors were all shining out of the skies like you know those fireworks we had when we were kids and we watched though, we took turns, and maybe someone fell asleep and we saw a little bit of I don't know a flicker of light or a bit of mist and we went over there and lo and behold we saw that someone had buried the body.

CREON: How is this possible?

HERM: Well not buried buried I mean no one dug a grave it wasn't six feet under or anything like that but it was a burial you could tell—the dirt was laid on the corpse the way you're supposed to all ritual like and there was a little bit of I don't know maybe it was some kind of—look all I know is, someone buried the body.

CREON: Who paid you?

HERM: Sir?

CREON: Who paid you to look the other way—all of you— who paid you to all pretend to be asleep or to all just conveniently somehow not see?

HERM: No sir. We did not. It's true we moved around a bit. It's true we shifted locations a little because the air oh sir the stench the stink oh sir you can understand what it was like when the wind started to blow in our direction oh man you have no idea what a rotting corpse can do to the smell of a sandwich when you're just trying to throw some food down your throat on a quick break but we took turns and someone was always looking and I dunno then there was this little disruption this maybe puff of smoke like in a magic act and sure enough we went over there and voila— body. Buried. Ritual. Supernatural like.

ZENO: How so?

HERM: Well there wasn't no signs you know that it was a human. And it wasn't an animal dug up the ground around it and managed to get dust on it and there weren't no tracks or nothing leading up to the body. And yet—you know. It looked all holy like. You know, the gods kinda intervened. Right?

ZENO: I knew there had to be something unearthly about it. The gods have got to be involved. No human could--

CREON: (to Zeno) You too? Are you stupid? Are you simply as dumb as you are ugly? There were no gods involved. This wasn't the work of anything divine—this was the work of some human. *(to Herm)* How much money?

HERM: I don't have any money sir.

CREON: How much money were you paid to let someone come and bury—

HERM: I swear to you sir—

CREON: Your swearing is about as reliable as everything else about you. Go back and find out who did this. Someone is responsible and I want answers.

HERM: But suppose that guy's right and it isn't a person—I mean, of course it's gotta be a person, I mean, yeah yeah someone did this and I gotta go get to the bottom of this.

CREON: See to it.   Bring back the guilty party and be quick about it. Otherwise.

HERM: Uh otherwise?

CREON: Otherwise I'm going to hold you responsible and have a confession tortured out of you

HERM: Uh uh uh uh now you know that kinda thing, they proved it don't work

CREON: Well maybe we'll just try one more time

HERM: I'm gonna bring back the guilty party and I'm innocent and I'm going to prove it.

CREON: See that you do.

HERM: I'm gone.

CREON: Good.

HERM: Ya know it's just that you're the judge and you're the jury here sir and it's an awful thing when ya know false judgment guides the judge.

CREON: Zeno, have him put in the slammer and put a new squad of sentries in place around the body.

ZENO: Uh.   Yes sir.

HERM: Wait wait wait uh uh uh I got my walking orders and I'm gonna bring back the guy who did this and yeah yeah I'm gone consider it done yep gone.

Herm starts off reluctantly.

CREON: Zeno. Double the guards around the camp. Make sure everything is locked up tight.   Gotta keep a lid on this.

Zeno nods and is off. Creon goes back to his headquarters tent. Herm turns to a refugee, flirts.

HERM: Yeah yeah. I'm gonna find him. I'm gonna find who did this. Yeah.   Huh.   Or maybe just maybe you won't see my pretty face around these parts again.

He trudges off to look for who or what buried the body.

SCENE. SHOCK AND AWE, HEARTS AND MINDS

A soothsayer goes through the camp. Hears the approach of Tiresias and her walking stick—and heads off out of her way.

Thunder. Or distant explosions. Tiresias uses her walking stick to feel around for a place to receive the oracle.

She lights an offering.   Listens for the message.   The frightening screeches of birds start up again.   The same terrifying birds as before—not any kind of simply loud bird sound, but an awful sound of killing, ripping, death.

TIRESIAS: Boy!   Boy!

Boy rushes to her.

BOY: Sir?

TIRESIAS: Who is here? Who is here, blocking the oracle?

BOY: There's no one.

TIRESIAS: Liar!   Tell me what you see.

BOY: I. No

TIRESIAS: Look!   Tell me.

BOY: It's too awful.

TIRESIAS: Birds dripping the grease of meat from their beaks.

BOY: Yes.

TIRESIAS: Clawing and raking at each other, scrambling to get at flesh—

BOY: I don't want to look anymore.

TIRESIAS: Are they taking the offering?

BOY: Don't make me look.

TIRESIAS: Look through your fingers. Do you see? They aren't. Are they?

BOY: No.

TIRESIAS: Ignoring their duty as messengers of the gods.

BOY: Yes.

TIRESIAS: Is the palm reader nearby?   The yarrow stick man? The crystal ball gazer.

BOY: Not now.

TIRESIAS: Do you know what was written over the temple at Delphi?

BOY: No.

TIRESIAS: "Nothing in excess." Come on, Boy. Take me home.

Boy nods and leads Tiresias away.

SCENE. THE TRUTH IS OUT

Herm returns, with his arm firmly gripping Antigone, leading her toward Creon's headquarters.

ANTIGONE: Don't touch me.

HERM: Yeah and oh sure how else am I supposed to get you to come along?

ANTIGONE: I have nothing to hide. And nothing to run from.

HERM: Uh-huh uh-huh says the girl who is sneaking around doing what she's been ordered not to do.

ANTIGONE: Woman. Not a girl.

HERM: Whatever. Hello! All you there. She's arrested. Anyone who sees her try to take off—

ANTIGONE: Stop it!

Creon hears the commotion, emerges from headquarters, followed by Zeno.

CREON: What's this? Soldier, get your hands off my niece.

HERM: I did what you asked and though I have to confess I wasn't going to—you know, I really have been doing a lot of confessing—anyway I was just going to take off and not bother coming back at all and I just went to get my knapsack because I had the nicest little bottle of jelly in there you know like the kind you used to get in little cheap cafes and I managed to keep it out of harm's way through all the battles not that I did much fighting I'm a sentry you know so what do I discover when I go back to where they're all guarding the corpse but—well no, first we moved downwind of the smell again and—anyway there she was, burying that body.   Again.

CREON: What's the meaning of this—

HERM: Caught her in the act—

CREON: Antigone—

HERM: So you was so mad the last time I thought well I'm not long for this world the way things are going but at least I went back to the others and said let's go get that ritual burial dust off the corpse, you know, set it out under the sun again and let the buzzards pick at it and I saw some hungry canine creature heading toward it too, not the kind of thing you'd expect wandering around, some sort of lapdog, but so we took the dust off the body— ohmygod was that awful, had to use a broom and gloves— and I don't know why, maybe some sound, I think it was thunder, maybe lightning a sign you know and the smell the smell oh you can't believe the smell but then all of a sudden a tornado or whattaya call it a dust devil or well you know what it's like out here now that it doesn't rain no more and then there was a shriek wild like a gang of coyotes ripping apart a neighbor's cat and there she was screeching and wailing and digging round the body with her bare hands and fingers and she's even got the three libations and she's doing the whole thing as if this sack of bones was a hero laying in honor. So we started to run toward her, and believe me I thought she was gonna run off—but she just stood there. And then. And then. So. I figured—well, not bringing back somebody is gonna get me dead. But bringing back the perp—and here she is— that's gonna get me a promotion. Ya know. So. Survival of the fittest, here we are.

CREON: You there. Is there even a whiff of truth to any of this?

ANTIGONE: I don't deny it.

CREON: Stop. Shh. Zeno, take the sentry away—

HERM: Herm's the name, by the way, in case you need it for papers to write up a citation of honor. Or write a check. Or—cash is fine.

CREON: Just—. Off you go. Keep this quiet. You hear?

HERM: Loud and clear, sir. Got any food you can spare?

Zeno ushers him out. Creon turns to Antigone.

CREON: Answer me. And be very careful how you answer. Do you hear? I'm giving you a chance to clear this up. I imagine there was some misunderstanding.

ANTIGONE: I understood.

CREON: Again. I want to caution you. Your answers matter now. So. I take it that you didn't know that this burial was forbidden. Right?

ANTIGONE: No. I knew.

CREON: I'll start again. When you answer—

ANTIGONE: There's no point in this game. I knew that you had given orders to not bury my brother. How could I not know? The news was everywhere.

CREON: You knew. And yet you defied me.

ANTIGONE: I did what was right.

CREON: I am the one who determines what is right. You dared to defy the law?

> *Zeno returns.*

ANTIGONE: Whose law? Not my law. Not the divine law.

CREON: *(to Zeno; Creon refuses to address Antigone)* And now she is a philosopher. Delightful.

ANTIGONE: Should I just humor you and pretend that you are the all-knowing guardian of Justice? When I see as plain as the nose on my face that the rules you are making defy anything that is decent, anything that has to do with common humanity?

CREON: What do you know of common humanity?

ANTIGONE: There are things that we all know to be true, things that were given us as humans, to honor, to follow.

Ways to live our life. They come from a much higher authority than you. They come from above, from on high, from the divine, from gods, from the inner workings of humankind, from the spirit, from whatever you want to call it. I don't know where they come from. I just know they are part of the DNA that elevates us from primitive cells. These laws weren't just made yesterday. They didn't emerge from someone's idea of power or control. Their source is a mystery—but they're what separates us out from the animals. What makes us human. Otherwise why not just eat and let eat, kill and let kill. These divine laws live for all time. They are inalienable rights—and we all know them.

CREON: *(to Zeno)* Now she's a lawyer, telling her ruler how to write the laws.

ANTIGONE: They do not need to be written down. And they do not need to be trumpeted by a tin-foil dictator or someone who thinks he is the only one who knows what is right.

CREON: *(to Zeno)* Just like a female to not understand what needs to be sacrificed for our freedom, how our laws keep us safe, how our nation must survive.

ANTIGONE: Your freedom, your laws, your nation—do I have any part in it?

CREON: *(to Zeno)* Listen to her. Just like her father. And clearly has learned nothing from the mess he created.

ZENO: She is definitely a spitfire.

ANTIGONE: If you make any petty civil laws that defy the higher laws of humanity, then you can rest assured they will be challenged and that you will not have a day's peace!

CREON: *(finally to Antigone)* I said the body was not to be buried.

ANTIGONE: Say his name.   My brother. Polynices.

CREON: And when I said the body was not to be buried, that is exactly what I meant.

ANTIGONE: I knew what you meant.   And I knew it to be wrong.

CREON: *(to Zeno)* She is going to argue with me!

ANTIGONE: I don't need to argue.   I buried my brother. I'm guilty.   I don't deny it.   And now you have to deal with it.

CREON: You have to deal with the fact that you committed the highest crime—treason. By honoring a traitor—

ANTIGONE: Who was the traitor? One brother killed another—

CREON: One died defending the state.

ANTIGONE: One died defending what was his rightful place.

CREON: One a hero, one a criminal.

ANTIGONE: So you tell me how Death will judge them. You tell me how Hades will sort this out. Which one is good. Which one is evil.

CREON: She's going to push me.

ANTIGONE: I am going to stand by my actions. I am going to honor a brother as a human. I am going to ignore and defy anything that is vengeful or indecent or that denies anyone a chance to everlasting peace. If my brother's body is not given proper treatment then my brother's soul is not laid to rest—

CREON: And now the religious mumbo jumbo—

ANTIGONE: If my brother is to roam the earth unsettled or bring curses down upon the city, then that is not a law that is wise. And your decree does nothing we should be proud of.

CREON: All the people who are free today because of me are very proud. And they know that my laws are wise—

ANTIGONE: They know that you have gone too far, and if they weren't all quaking in their boots they would tell you.

Esme rushes on.

ESME: Antigone—stop—

CREON: Ah yes, the other thorn in my side. The other parasite, the other spawn, orphaned by profane parents, eating my food, living off my kindness—

ANTIGONE: It's done, Esme. Go away while you can—

CREON: So you plotted together and now you're both going to be queens of the underworld, brides of hell—

ANTIGONE: It was only me—

ESME: I was there. She was not alone—

ANTIGONE: I did the work. All by myself. Let the dead speak, because they know the truth.

ESME: No. Stop it. I helped, we did it together—

ANTIGONE: Stop taking credit. Your choice was to live. Mine was to die. Period. So live.

ESME: I was wrong I was just trying to stop you from putting yourself in danger I didn't

ANTIGONE: Even your voice is grating on me now.

ESME: I don't want to be alone—

ANTIGONE: You've got our sainted uncle. Let him rule you and your day.

ESME: Please don't be hateful please don't say what you will regret--

CREON: Take them both out of here. Lock them up.

ZENO: Yes sir.

> *Zeno starts to take Antigone and Esme away. Creon grabs Esme.*

CREON: No. You stay here.   No need to have the two of you plotting.

Zeno leads Antigone out. Creon turns to Esme.

Know when you are winning—and when anything else you do will lead you to lose.

ESME: Uncle, you cannot carry this out.

CREON: I did not make these laws to see them broken.

ESME: You cannot kill my sister.

CREON: A law that shows favoritism isn't worth the paper it's printed on.

ESME: She is going to marry your son.

CREON: I doubt that very much.

ESME: They love each other. They are made for each other. Since they were children they've been like intertwining vines in a garden—

CREON: He'll have plenty more fertile fields to plow.

ESME: Please, Uncle. King Creon. Please, I beg of you—. Let her go.   Let her live to carry your grandchildren into a new world—

CREON: I have had it up to here with the bloodsuckers today! Go! Get out of here. Wait until I call you. Just be glad you're not in chains.

Esme leaves. Reluctant.

SCENE. THE SEDUCTION OF PEACE

Eurydice appears. Goes to Creon.   She touches him, his cheek, his lips, his brow.

EURYDICE: You are warm, love. Your face is hot. You aren't well.

CREON: I'm fine.

EURYDICE: There is too much going on. Let me rub your palms, let me massage your temples.   I've saved some scented oil—blood orange and verbena.   Let me take care of you, just a moment.

Creon gives in—for a tiny moment. Then breaks away.

CREON: Later, my dear one.   Not now.

EURYDICE: What is the point of being in charge, of having all this power, if you cannot take a moment to enjoy just taking a breath, just being with your wife?

CREON: That is why I do all of this.   For us.

EURYDICE: Then think of us, love.   Think of us.

CREON: I do.

EURYDICE: I'm thinking of our son.   I'm thinking of how his life will be—.

CREON: His life will be fine. He is the son of a warrior, of the commander of armies, of the ruler of Thebes. He has nothing to fear.

EURYDICE: I'm thinking of how his life will be. If you.

CREON: If I what—?   If I what?!   My own wife—   Going against me—

EURYDICE: I would never. I would never. I want what's best for you.   I want to be your Queen. I want us to live a long and happy life.

CREON: Then leave me alone.   Go away. Let me forget what just happened.   Let me believe I have a loyal wife—

EURYDICE: You do—

CREON: Go.

EURYDICE: Love—

CREON: Go.   Please.   Didn't I get you a little pup to take your mind off all of this?   Go and find it. Go.

She heads off, angrily. Creon is alone.

SCENE. PENANCE

A makeshift guardhouse in the encampment. Zeno and a guard (Herm) keep an eye on Antigone. She is a caged animal. [Could be created by a sculpted circle of light. Doesn't require walls, bars.]

Zeno knows she isn't going anywhere. He drops his guard as a soldier for a moment. He steps away from the makeshift prison. He looks out at the ruined land.

ZENO: There were small market stalls right around here. On weekends, the farmers would come in from all around with heaps of all kinds of fresh produce. The colors, that's what I loved the most. Yellows, purple, really bright green. Deepest blueberries. Somehow I remember radishes with white stripes on them. Is that right, I wonder?

GUARD/HERM: Oh yeah uh-huh they could have stripes.

ZENO: Never liked radishes much. Just thought they were pretty. The color.

GUARD/HERM: And there was the nice lady you know who would cut up a pear, you know, maybe slice a peach or a tomato, and give me a sample and yeah that was cool, 'course she was just trying to drum up business, tempt me and all.

ZENO: Still. It tasted good. And. Down the way, closer to the water, that's where we went to school.

GUARD/HERM: Oh you went to the nice place that was pretty nice. Not me. I was at the school on the other side of the hill. Yeah not so great, not such a great school. But I had friends.

ZENO: Yeah. I had friends. *(referring to Antigone)* She's like her father. Always goes too far.

GUARD/HERM: There ya go ya know, some people just don't know when to shut up. Always making trouble.

ZENO: Wouldn't mind if the trouble was just for herself alone. But she gets everybody else involved, too.

GUARD/HERM: Stirring everybody up yeah.

ZENO: Suppose we just want to have a normal life.

GUARD/HERM: Suppose we just want to ya know keep a low profile, let things just go on cruise for a while.

ZENO: Yeah. It would be nice if we could all just—well. Just. Normal.

GUARD/HERM: So what do ya, so what's gonna happen, you know, what are they gonna do to her? I mean, well, what should WE do?

ZENO: **You** don't do anything. Got it? *(goes to Antigone)* You're stubborn. Haven't you ever learned to just bide your time, just try to go along to get along.

ANTIGONE: I didn't have the chance.

ZENO: Oh wait, where's my tiny violin?

> *Antigone ignores his sarcasm. Remembers the land.*

ANTIGONE: It was a beautiful city, wasn't it? Your school—there were apple trees in the yard.

ZENO: Once.

ANTIGONE: We would ride out into the country to look at the lavender farms, then, on the way back, we'd see the city glowing in the distance, and beyond that, the water, going on forever, and little boats with twinkling lights bobbing here and there.

ZENO: I never did that.

ANTIGONE: I miss it.

ZENO: Yeah. I get it.

ANTIGONE: I miss the people. Friends. Neighbors.

ZENO: Your family.

ANTIGONE: I washed each one of them after they died. I followed all the rituals, used the exact correct cloth, the herb-scented water, the lotions, the spices. I covered their eyes with gold-embossed coins. I poured the libations—all three, just as it is required. Holy water from a sacred jug. I don't even know if I believe in all the religious texts or teachings. Who is god or what is god and which god is the only god---I have no idea. But I know what is right, and I know it is not right for a human to be carrion for wild animals, feral cats, and little pink-rhinestone-collared creatures we petted in our laps and washed with oatmeal shampoo and have now gone wild, we cannot let them turn on my brother, and carry his blood-crusted limbs around as food.

ZENO: There was a law—

ANTIGONE: It's the dirty work, you know.   Cleaning the bodies.   Doing the burial rites.   It's the unclean job. That's why it's done by women.

ZENO: If you say so.

ANTIGONE: I don't care if you agree. Just try to understand.

ZENO: So. Your family—all gone.

ANTIGONE: Yes.

ZENO: Well. You did right by your brother. At least you have that for comfort.

ANTIGONE: That much. Yes. I have that. Nothing else. No one left to mourn me.

   In the distance, faint sound of waves.

Oh. The sea.   Listen.

ZENO: Too far. Can't hear it from here.

ANTIGONE: If the wind is right, if the waves are large enough—

   Esme appears, in a vision. Antigone sees her. Zeno does not. Nor does he hear her.

ESME: You always forget.

ANTIGONE: You shouldn't be here.

ESME: Right. So I'm not.

ZENO: Someone's gotta guard you. Not that you're going anywhere.

ANTIGONE: True.

ESME: I'll just sit with you awhile.

ANTIGONE Good.

ZENO: Whatever.

ESME: Good.

ANTIGONE: I don't want to die.

ESME: I know.

ZENO: Should have thought of that earlier.

ANTIGONE: Still. If I must.

ZENO: Yeah. Just don't pull anything.

ANTIGONE: I never really wanted to die.

> *Haemon may appear here, in a vision, holding his hand out to her, even perhaps kissing her.*

ESME: Shhh.

ZENO: Yeah. It's a bum rap.

ANTIGONE: But I will.

ZENO: *(to Herm)* Watch her. She's trouble. But. Just watch.

Zeno leaves. Antigone sits in silence. Esme hovers nearby.

Herm glances over at Antigone. He approaches her. Threateningly. She gives him a look. He stops. Backs off.

SCENE.   REASON VERSUS TYRANNY

Haemon enters his father's headquarters.   Creon is there, with Zeno by his side.

CREON: You too? Come to tell me that I should let that woman get the best of me?

HAEMON: The best of you cannot be taken away, father. I was lucky enough to be raised by you, to know what it was like to be the child of a great man.

CREON: So you haven't taken sides against me.

HAEMON: I have always been on your side. I will always be on your side. Everything I do is to support you and all that is great about you.

CREON: A father doesn't want his son to betray him.

HAEMON: A son wants the same thing.

CREON: So you're fine that I have interrupted your plans for a wedding.

HAEMON: A wedding is not something to worry about in times like these.

CREON: Good.   Solid thinking. You understand that to restore order is our only hope—if we're ever to return to a decent world.   A city where people feel safe on the streets, where they don't have to fear for their lives.   A place where we are all striving to make our nation strong. Where we can sort out good and evil, right from wrong. Where our enemies understand there is no place for them here and we will root them out and destroy them. You'll stand with me against our enemies, won't you?

HAEMON: I have always sworn to protect our people from any danger.

CREON: That's my son. Wise. Strong. (beat) You know the thing about women—and love.   Well. I was young once. You think you are in love with someone forever, and then you realize, you are just in love with love. And one love is as good as another, isn't it?   It's all glorious, all brilliant, all soul-consuming when you first meet the girl you think is the girl of your dreams—those hot afternoons in bed with the sun boiling the windows and you're covered with sweat and the scent of juices from your bodies and your lips are numb and you're about to pass out in the heat and you don't even care, you're so caught up in the fire of the moment.   And then one day, bleh. It's just an afternoon gone ordinary.   Cold day, hot day, doesn't matter. You're just going through the motions. She could be anybody. She's not even interested.   You don't need to be there.

HAEMON: Father. I am sworn to follow your decisions. We don't need to talk about love.

CREON: Fine. Fine. Sometimes a father just wants to shoot the breeze with his son, but. Fine. Let me tell you this. We make hard choices because otherwise there is no civilization. No one is safe. There are riots in the street and confusion and harm. When anarchy reigns, humans are doomed. Why? Because humans are weak. If left to their own devices, what would they do? Where would they be? People need discipline. Just like children—they need to learn respect and order. Otherwise everyone is stealing from everyone else, or lying around on beaches, or coveting their neighbor's wife and his manservant and his maidservant, and burning down each other's gas stations and grocery stores. Or just letting everything go all to hell. And women are the worst. They have no concept of discipline. Respect. Order. They'd run hog wild if we'd let them. Nothing would get done. They're the weakest of the weak and we can't let them push us around. Never. There'd be no world as we know it if we would have let women have their way. We'd all be dead. We'd all go to the dogs. That is why a woman should never ever get the best of us. We are men. Let's remember that. No matter what.

HAEMON: Yes, sir.

CREON: Duty and honor. We know our duty. Just as our citizens know their duty. And follow me. They know I have integrity. And want what is best for them.

HAEMON: Yes sir. I honor you as my father. And I have duties as your son.

CREON: Good.

HAEMON: And one of those duties is to look out for you, to see what perhaps is being hidden from you. To see what's going on around us—to listen and hear what perhaps the people are afraid to say when you are near.

CREON: Well, you won't find anything if you pursue that line of inquiry.

HAEMON: Father. They are terrified.

CREON: Of course they are. Look at this world. Suicide bombers. Police out of control. Can't get on a train or stroll through a park without fear of being blown up by terrorist madmen anywhere in this world.

HAEMON: They are terrified of you.

CREON: Ha.

HAEMON: The entire city is terrified of a man who would put his own niece to death—just because she wanted to pay honor to a fallen brother. Just because she didn't want to see his body putrefy in the streets. They have had enough death. Their hearts ache for this young woman who just wants to take a decent action. They understand her. They think she is acting on behalf of all that's holy.

CREON: They're delusional. You're delusional.

HAEMON: They wonder what kind of terrorist madman is leading them. If he will subject his own relative to such a horrible punishment—then what would he do to them?

CREON: They understand there has to be order. They'll follow me.

HAEMON: And yet, why?

CREON: I am the rightful king.

HAEMON: They never voted for you. You became their ruler because someone else died—and it passed to you. Why should they be loyal?

CREON: I should have known. I should have known. This entire meeting with me is about you wanting to get up that whore's skirt. Driven by your dick just like the lowliest foot soldier in the world's worst army. You'll say anything.

HAEMON: I'm trying to protect you. You're acting out of anger. It's impulsive. It's rage. You aren't thinking. You aren't seeing consequences. You've traded reason for a hair trigger. No one will want to follow you if you keep this up.

CREON: I fought in wars! And I should let a whiny little baby tell me how to rule—

HAEMON: Fine. Get mad at me, hurl insults, whatever you need to do to get over this crazy mood—. Listen. You know what it's like when a flood comes, when there are torrents of rain and wind. How do the trees along the riverbank survive? They bend. Their trunks, their branches, give way, and they bow in the wind in order to ride out the gale. If they are rigid, they break in half. Roots separating from the rest. If a ship goes through a hurricane with taut sails, it will be picked up and tossed. Capsizing. Ending upside down. But if the sails are loose.... You need to bend. Not be rigid. Stop this idea of executing Antigone because she just wanted to bury a body.

CREON: Not a body. A traitor. What she did is a crime.

HAEMON: The people of Thebes do not think so.

CREON: So I'm going to be ruled by the people of Thebes.

HAEMON: Yes. Together you make the laws.

CREON: Are you out of your mind? I am the ruler. I make the laws.

HAEMON: Do you hear yourself? You sound like a tantrum-crazy child!

CREON: How is there any order, if it doesn't come from me?

HAEMON: No government comes from only one man.

CREON: I'm in charge. The city belongs to me.

HAEMON: Better go be king of a desert then. That's all you're fit for.

CREON: You'll turn on me, your own father, because you're the pawn of a woman.

HAEMON: I'm no one's pawn.

CREON: You'll let a woman lead you around by the nose—

HAEMON: You've got to stop all this brutality—

CREON: —brutality! you haven't seen brutality yet!

HAEMON: I'm trying to get you to see the truth—

CREON: I see the truth and I see you're pathetic—

HAEMON: Talk and talk and talk and insult me, fine—

CREON: — letting a woman have your way with you—

HAEMON: —just let justice be your gu—

CREON: —questioning me, saying the woman is right—

HAEMON: Woman, man, what's the difference who is right—

CREON: —letting some itch cloud your judgment—

HAEMON: —I'm trying to stop you from being a tyrant! Sieg heil!

Haemon flashes the Nazi salute. Creon explodes.

CREON: Oh you'll pay for that. That's it. No more stalling. That criminal dies today. Bring her here. The bride of hell will die in front of the boy who is lucky his father rescued him from having to be a bridegroom to—

HAEMON: You will not do this—

CREON: And how are you going to stop me?

They face off. Beat.

HAEMON: Take a good look. Because this is the last you'll ever see of me.

Haemon storms off. Creon turns to Zeno.

CREON: I'm not the man now. Antigone is the man.

ZENO: Your son seems—. He may be desperate.

CREON: Bring the criminals here.

ZENO: Criminals?

CREON: My nieces. Get them ready for execution—

ZENO: Both of them? The sister? Esme, too? That—well, we don't want the people rising up crying murder, sir?

CREON: There is no murder in war.

ZENO: No. But. Peace—

CREON: Fine. Right. Peace. Peace. Right. Right. Antigone only will be sentenced. She is in love with death—let her be a bride of Hades. Let her wedding in the underworld be witnessed by restless souls wandering in the dark. (beat) I'll bury her alive.

ZENO: Sir—

CREON: Take her up a steep path. Find a cave to be her tomb. Dark, like the eternal night she's about to enjoy. Put in just enough food so that her so-called gods are appeased. Don't want any curses raining down on the city. If she prays hard enough and long enough maybe Hades himself will show up and save her.

Zeno nods. He heads toward the guardhouse.

SCENE. THE FUNERAL DIRGE

Zeno escorts Antigone through the camp.

Eurydice and refugees gather and watch.

EURYDICE/REFUGEES: Love how do we fight you
Love how do we stop you
How do we keep you from ruling us
And leading us astray
And yet love we can't touch you
Love we can't see you
Love we can't name you
Love we can't even say what you are
You drive us all to madness
You take away our reason
Blind us to what is right and what is law
Love you're a killer
Love you're a lover
Love come be with us
Once again

> *Eurydice can't take her eyes off Antigone. Antigone tries to be fearless.*

ANTIGONE: Who would have thought that even the rubble of this camp would be dear to me now that I know I won't be seeing it again. Maybe I see what was once here, maybe I can taste the salt of the ocean breeze, breathe in the scents of the spices cooking in the neighboring kitchens, hear the rhythmic drone of music coming faintly from the windows.

ZENO: I don't know.

ANTIGONE: When I was younger, no matter how upside down and crazy my family seemed, I just assumed I'd finish out my life with children, with Haemon as my husband. I thought we might go somewhere else, where no one knew us, and we'd both work to make a life for ourselves—one that wasn't driven by the families we were born into. Maybe we'd have a little cantina decorated with sea shells and sell lunch to hungry tourists looking for a friendly place to sit. Maybe we'd be teachers and inspire our students to love the geography of river valleys and the movement of the stars.

ZENO: Maybe. But then you wouldn't be famous. Then no one would come out of their hiding place to watch you march to glory.

ANTIGONE: Is that what I'm doing?

ZENO: Look at them. All of them. Watching you. Wishing they had the nerve.

ANTIGONE: Who was it—it was Niobe. She was sentenced to a living death like me but was turned into a stone, the Weeping Rock, with ivy sprouting all around her, tears flowing forever.

ZENO: Niobe was a god.

ANTIGONE: I know. No need to mock me. No divine intervention. I get that. Thanks. I'm just trying to keep myself company. I'm going to be sealed in a tomb, my breath sucked away a little at a time. Halfway in this world, halfway in the next. All because of who I am. Who my father was. The curse of the house of Laius. The curse of the house of Oedipus. My father is my brother. My mother Jocasta wed her son.

ZENO: They didn't know—

ANTIGONE: And all of us children—well, the curse ends here. I wept for them all, by the way. I wailed and tore my dress and made sure that the heavens and earth and all of hell knew that they were loved. Love matters. Love is all. And now, it's the only light I have.

> *Creon appears, watches as Antigone is led up into the rocks.*

CREON: If people could always sing their own funeral songs, there'd never be any death—because the song would never end.

ANTIGONE: A light I have to carry in memory, because there is none here now.

CREON: *(calling to Zeno)* I said take her away quickly. Before this goes on too long. She made a choice. Wall her into the cave. Pile on the stones. She chose darkness, not light.

> *Creon spots Eurydice, her eyes fixed on Antigone.*

EURYDICE: Wind is coming up. I fear her soul is being tossed in a storm.

CREON: You don't need to be out here.

EURYDICE: And yet she goes on.

CREON: Don't watch her.

EURYDICE: It's cold all of a sudden.

CREON: It's fine.

EURYDICE: Shadow over the sun. Leaves turning down. She doesn't even flinch. She keeps going.

CREON: Shh.

EURYDICE: Birds calling. Dogs barking.

CREON: It's just the wind.

> *He tries to pull her away; she will not stop watching.
> Creon finds himself alone. Abandoned.*

SCENE. THE WILL OF THE GODS. DIVINE INTERVENION. REASON AND LAW CAN ONLY GO SO FAR BECAUSE THE RANDOM ORDER OF THE UNIVERSE TAKES OVER ANYWAY...OR??

Thunder. Lightning. Wind.

Tiresias is led by Boy to Creon.

CREON: Now is not a good time

TIRESIAS: When is it ever?

CREON: I must say, you're looking quite—lovely today.

TIRESIAS: Do not play with me. I'm not in the mood.

CREON: The attitude! You do know who you're talking to—

TIRESIAS: Yes. The man whose city I have saved over and over. The man who has power this very moment because of me—

CREON: You didn't fight in the war.

TIRESIAS: You know exactly what I mean.

CREON: Alright.

TIRESIAS: Say it.

Creon says nothing.

Let's go, Boy. This is a waste of time.

CREON: Fine. Fine. Your oracles and prophecies guided us to victory. You provided the answer to mysteries. You showed us how to triumph over our enemies.

TIRESIAS: Just so we know where we stand.

CREON: I am grateful. I get it.

TIRESIAS: Perhaps not. Because you are standing on the razor's edge.

CREON: Oh I can't stand your riddles. My blood runs cold. Why do you have this effect on me?

TIRESIAS: Maybe it's my perfume.

CREON: What do you want?

TIRESIAS: A favor. And if you don't grant it, you've heard the last from me.

CREON: Tell me.

TIRESIAS: Stop this. Stop this nonsense.

CREON: What nonsense—

TIRESIAS: Stop this execution. You've ruined my oracles. You are calling a horrific curse down upon us all.

CREON: I have already given the order—

TIRESIAS: Oh and an order can't be taken back?

CREON: Not by me.

TIRESIAS: You've heard the screeching of birds, you've heard the screams in the night.   Tell him, Boy. Tell him what has gone on.

Boy just stands there, tongue-tied.

Fine. I will fill you in.   You know my calling is to read the signs. I sit in my stone chair and the signs come to me. Well, the signs are not being sent.   I light an offering fire and the fire goes out. The flame turns to smoke and dies away. Because of you. There is no message from the heaven-sent birds.   I listen and listen to their calls and they are all wrong.   It's not the sound of the gods, it's not a message with any content. It is clashing and squalling and ripping and tearing.   The boy tells me.   They are not diving toward the smoke of the divine with news for us— they are screeching through the air with fat dripping from their beaks, with the flesh of a dead man stuck in their talons, with the aim to kill each other over rotting meat. Because of you. No desire to tell us what we need to know to survive. No grace. No mercy. Just dripping guts and oozing slime. Because of you. The boy here saw it. He tells me—and he even leaves out the awful parts, but I know. I know what is going on. The oracle has failed. The signs have been cut off. Because of you.

CREON: That's it. Enough of this craziness and blame today. Guards. Someone. Get her out of here.

TIRESIAS: Call off the curses!

CREON: That's how you people thrive, isn't it? You so-called soothsayers. Phony oracles. Scare us all with fake talk of doom and what will befall us. It's all about making money, isn't it? You psychics—there's no money in pleasantries or nice birthday wishes. But fill our heads with all the things that are going to go wrong and we'll fill your tip jar up with more and more cash. NO! Get out of here. I'm sick of what bribes and greed have done to all our people. And you should especially be ashamed of yourself—manufacturing terrifying prophecies for a profit. You're all alike.

TIRESIAS: I should make you eat those words—

CREON: What's the matter? No good disasters to predict, no alms to beg from people wanting to know the day of their death.

TIRESIAS: —but I'll admit—I have a vested interest in this place.

CREON: See? All about money—

TIRESIAS: I'm not talking about finances. I'm talking about not wanting to further harm the city I've had to protect for how many hundred years? I've come to like it here— though at present I'm glad I can't see what it's become. Thank you, gods, for that.

CREON: I'm not going to give in to any charlatan who is just trying to profit from tragedy.

TIRESIAS: Oh really. What will you do with your curse?

CREON: There's no curse—

TIRESIAS: There's always a curse. There will always be a curse. Until we can figure out how to be true humanity, truly humane, the curses will go on. Just have to figure out which one. This one I know I can stop.

CREON: How?

TIRESIAS: Surrender the dead to the mourners and the wailers. Stop using his corpse as an unwinnable war between pride and destiny, power and love, revenge and forgiveness. Pull the vultures and the jackals off the body. How does any of this prove you are strong? There's no point in killing him more than once. Take my advice.

CREON: Take the advice of a crackpot masquerading as a priest—

TIRESIAS: Take me away, Boy. I don't have the energy for this. I'm an old man.

CREON: Not anymore you aren't.

TIRESIAS: I'll be through with this near-death sentence soon enough. The elephant doesn't forget.

Boy leads Tiresias off.

I was quite an archer in my day, boy. Did I ever tell you that? Oh. Just one moment.

She turns back to Creon.

TIRESIAS (cont.): You know, I have a full quiver of poison darts. And one more special little arrow. I've saved it for you: Get ready for the wailing chants and loud laments of men and women shrieking in mourning. Get ready for ten thousand hearts to be aligned against you in hate. Get ready for the wild hounds and beasts and crows to visit your family, get ready to fight off the dogs as they grab for the mutilated limbs of the ones you love as the sun beats down on the rotting corpses. The doggies have a taste for human meat, now. Can you really stop them? Coming soon. Coming to a place near you. Feel it? See the wind? See the storm clouds? I can. That much I can see.

Come on, boy. Let him figure it out himself.

Lightning. Darkness passes over. Thunder or the roar of cannons or bombs—it doesn't matter.

SCENE.   FEAR THE CURSE.

Tiresias is gone. Creon is shaken. Zeno turns to him.

ZENO: She's gone, sir.

CREON: He.

ZENO: He. His prophecies—. That was. What should we—

CREON: Quiet. Nothing.

ZENO: I'm pretty sure he never made a prediction, never read a sign, that wasn't right for the city.

CREON: There is always a first time.

ZENO: Sir.

CREON: Isn't there?

ZENO: I'm a gambler. But I wouldn't take the odds on that one.

CREON: No. I know. I—.   No.

ZENO: Let Antigone go free. Let her out of the tomb.   And build one instead for the body of her brother.   Pull off the ravens and the dogs by hand if you have to.   Stop the whole cycle of death.

CREON: It's. Not possible.

ZENO: I don't mean to be disrespectful, sir.

CREON: I gave an order.

102

ZENO: Take it back.

CREON: Can I just—?

ZENO: Take it back? Yes. As fast as you can. Before anything else goes wrong. Before any other tragedy rains down upon us. Don't tempt fate.

CREON: I can't bear to look weak, to call off my own law. It goes against everything I stand for.

ZENO: Stand for something else then.

CREON: I know you are right. I feel it.

ZENO: Do it now. I'll go with you. Don't send anyone else in your place—we'll take care of this and make sure it gets done.

CREON: Yes. I'll go. I'll do it.

ZENO: That is a sign of strength.

> *The sounds of the screeching birds grows louder. Zeno and Creon head off.*
>
> *Thunder. Lightning. Frightening noise and light.*
>
> *The people in the encampment begin a crazy dance.*
>
> *They could dance without words or making unintelligible sounds or they could repeat an almost unintelligible chant over and over, which could be a single word or another language entirely.*
>
> *Their sounds soon drown out the birds.*

The chant grows louder. The dance grows more manic.

There could be dervishes.   Flagellants.   Anything.

It's a dance to Dionysus.   It's a Bacchic ritual.

Except this time, it's just frenzy—no one dies.

Louder and faster, they keep dancing and chanting.

[OR: Another option: Bodies appear in shadows, running, hurling rocks at Antigone in the cave as if they are the mountain burying her alive.]

Lightning.   More lightning. Thunder.

In the midst of it, we see Antigone, in her cave, twirling her long scarf through her fingers.

In shadows and flashes of lightning we see Haemon in a vision, or Haemon seeing Antigone.

Lights and shadows continue to flash; we see Antigone wrap the scarf around her neck, and Haemon with a knife.

We see the two of them in a dance of death.

Lightning.   Thunder.   Wind.

Suddenly it all STOPS.

SCENE.   FEAR THE WORST

Zeno enters.   Something about him makes everyone and everything go still and silent.

ZENO: Friends. Citizens. I have news.

It is hard for him to speak.

ZENO (cont.): Soothsayers can read the signs.
Interpret the messages.
Sometimes.
Sometimes the signs come too late.

Zeno falters. Goes on.

The king—.
The king is alive.

If it is alive to walk and breathe but to have all come to ashes all around—

Where is Creon's wife? I must tell her first.

Eurydice comes through the camp.   She looks at Zeno.

EURYDICE: You have news for me.

ZENO: Yes.

EURYDICE: You do not have good news for me.

ZENO: No.

EURYDICE: Antigone is dead.

ZENO: Yes.

EURYDICE: My husband—

ZENO: No. He lives. Antigone is dead.   By her own hand.
And.

EURYDICE: And.

>   *She waits. Zeno goes on.*

ZENO: When we got to the cave where Antigone was
walled up, we heard faint cries and moaning from inside.
Creon said, hurry, help me, that is my son's voice, help me.
We pulled rocks away as fast as we could. That is my son's
voice, Creon kept saying. That is Haemon, wailing, crying
out. As soon as the opening was large enough, Creon
crawled into the cave—there was still no light, barely
enough air, but he climbed inside. I followed.   There we
saw Haemon. Holding on to Antigone. Wailing her name.
She had taken her scarf.   She had wound it around her
neck. And hung herself.   She was dangling in the cave
with Haemon clutching her, holding her as if he would
never let go.   She was not going to die by anyone's decree
except her own. And Haemon—. Creon called to him,
tried to go to him to comfort him. But Haemon drew his
sword.

>   *Eurydice just stands and listens.*

>   *Antigone can be seen, watching along with Death, in
>   the Underworld.*

As Zeno speaks, Creon appears, stumbling in shock and grief, carrying/dragging the lifeless body of his son.

Creon dodged the sword. Haemon looked at him. Then, your son plunged the sword into his own beating heart. Blood. Blood. He grabbed his bride again and held her, the blood draining out of his wounds, the blood spurting out of his mouth. His final kiss to her. Sealed in blood.

Creon arrives in front of Eurydice. He gently lays the body of Haemon in front of her. She is deadly silent. Motionless.

When Creon finally speaks, his words are barely a mumble.

CREON: My wife...

Eurydice goes to her son. She looks at his dead body. She dips her fingers in his blood and rubs the blood all over herself.

CREON: Eurydice...

He reaches for her, as if begging for comfort. Begging for a touch. Eurydice pushes him away. She tenderly caresses her son's face, his hands, his arms.

CREON: My dearest...

Eurydice ignores Creon. She focuses on her son. Then: she pulls something from the body of Haemon. Turns to Creon.

EURYDICE: You've done this. You created this world of fear and hate.

> *She takes the object she pulled from Haemon and raises it. Zeno rushes to protect Creon.*

ZENO: She's got a knife—!

EURYDICE: You live with it.

> *But Zeno's warning is too late. And misdirected. Eurydice slashes the blade across her neck, hard. Her blood spurts everywhere.   She collapses. Gasping.*

CREON: Noooooooooooooooo

> *Creon goes to her fallen body. Eurydice convulses. And is dead.*

CREON: No

ZENO: She's gone.

CREON: (barely audible) ohmygod ohmygod ohmygod

> *Shrieks and wails are heard from around the camp.*

ohmygodohmygodohmygod

ZENO: Too late for god

> *Creon falls to his knees holding the body of Eurydice. He starts rocking back and forth, his words a barely audible mantra.*

CREON: death take me death take me

ZENO: That's the future. Now we've got to deal with the present

CREON: all gone all gone

ZENO: Stop

CREON: death take me death take me

ZENO: We've got work to do.

CREON: no one left to mourn with me   praying praying for death to take me   praying just for death

ZENO: Then don't pray at all.

> *Creon is broken. Beaten. Sounds of mourning, or the wind, or silence. He is motionless. Frozen in grief.*
>
> *Zeno leads Creon off.*
>
> *Antigone continues her vigil in the Underworld.*

SCENE. EPILOGUE.

Lights start to fade. The faint sound of waves.

Esme appears.

ESME: All gone? No one left?
Did you forget about me?
Too bad.
I'm still here.

And this—
And this—
And this isn't over.

> *Esme stands in a pool of light as everyone else disappears.*
>
> *Images appear of migrants from all over the world, boat people, war, mass graves—from the Vietnam era through Rwanda, Bosnia, Somalia, Syria today.*
>
> *Images appear of liberation movements, social justice movements, from near past to today. Fists raised in resistance. One after another.*
>
> *Blackout. End of play.*

Printed in the USA
CPSIA information can be obtained
at www.ICGtesting.com
LVHW051545260124
769786LV00001B/69